For Aaron Sekora, with love.

THE
SHEEPISH BOOK OF
OPPOSITES

By George Mendoza
Illustrated by Kathleen Reidy

Publishers · GROSSET & DUNLAP · New York

Library of Congress Catalog Card Number: 81-84017. ISBN: 0-448-12039-9.
Text copyright © 1982 by Ruth Sekora. Illustrations copyright © 1982 by Kathleen Reidy.
All rights reserved. Published simultaneously in Canada. Printed in the United States of America.

HELLO

A shepherd leads a special kind of life. He is always watching over and protecting his flock of sheep.

A shepherd sees everything. He sees his sheep...

YOUNG

OLD

COMING

GOING

WET

DRY

WAKING

SLEEPING

IN

OUT

HAPPY

SAD

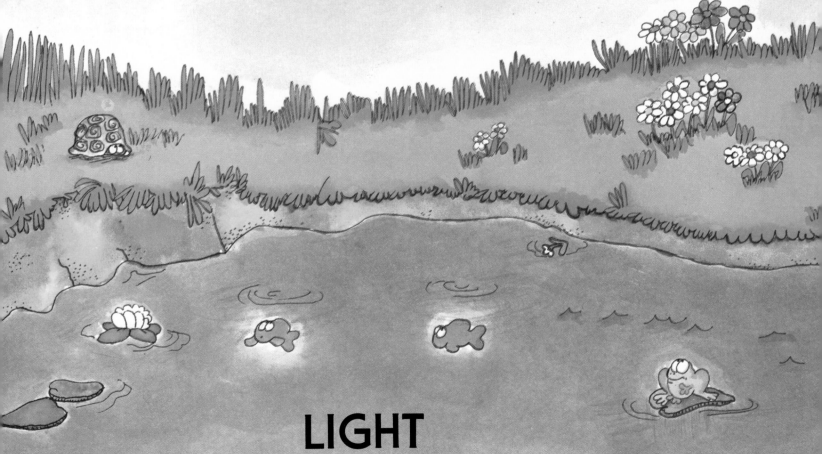

LIGHT

HEAVY

UP

DOWN

SITTING

STANDING

LITTLE

BIG

FRONT

BACK

NEAR

FAR

HOT

COLD

NOISY

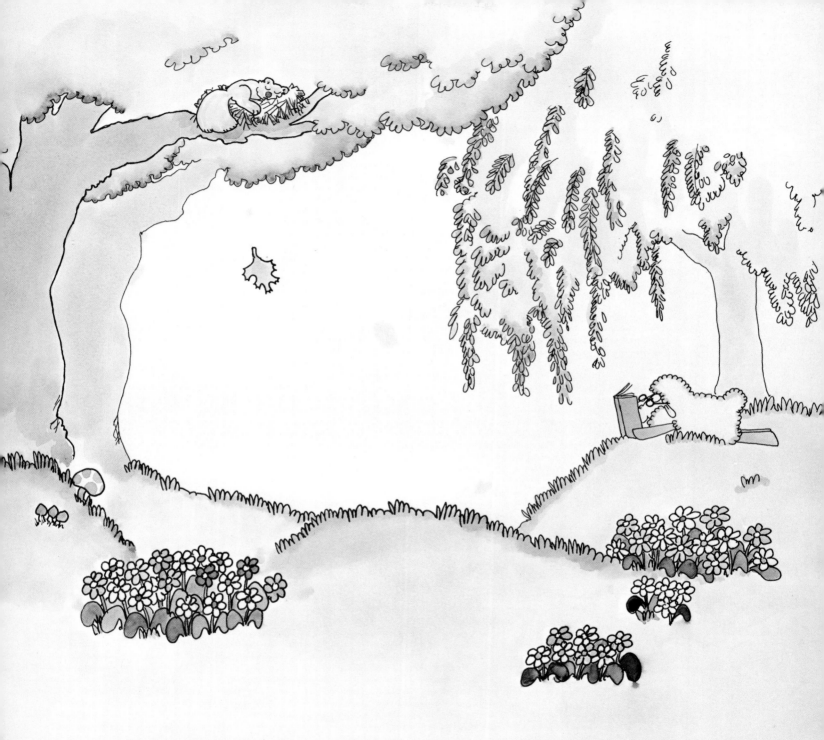

QUIET

FAST

SLOW

Sheep may all appear the SAME to you...

But to a shepherd, sheep are all DIFFERENT...

GOODBYE